# BLAZE
### AND THE MONSTER MACHINES™

# CATCH CRUSHER!

By **Frank Berrios** • Illustrated by **Dynamo Limited**

Based on the teleplay "Tool Duel!" by **Dustin Ferrer**

A Random House PICTUREBACK® Book

Random House 🏠 New York

D1275130

Early one morning, Blaze and AJ drove into Gabby's garage. The big truck didn't look so good.

"Gabby! We need your help!" said AJ. "Something's wrong with Blaze."

"What's the matter, Blaze?" asked Gabby.

"It's really strange," replied Blaze. "Something inside me keeps making a funny noise. Here, listen." Blaze revved his engine, and they all heard an odd squeak.

"The sound's coming from your transmission, Blaze," said Gabby. "I'm going to need my tools to look inside. Every tool I could ever need is in my toolbox."

Using her wrench, Gabby quickly found the problem. A rubber duck was stuck in Blaze's engine!

"A rubber ducky! I wonder how that got in there!" giggled Blaze.

Just then, more Monster Machines roared into the garage. They needed repairs, too!

"Don't worry," said Gabby. "As long as I have my toolbox, I can fix anything!"

Peeking through the window of Gabby's garage, Crusher and Pickle listened to what the friends were saying.

"I wish I had a toolbox like that!" said Crusher. "When no one's looking, I'm gonna take it!"

"Crusher, you can't do that!" said Pickle. But it was too late. Crusher raced off with Gabby's toolbox!

Gabby was ready to start the repairs. "Okay, everyone. I'll just grab my tools and we'll get to fixin'," she said. But her toolbox was gone!

Blaze and AJ spotted Pickle and Crusher driving away with the toolbox. "Don't worry, Gabby," said Blaze. "AJ and I will get those tools back."

Crusher happily drove up a hill with the toolbox on his back and Pickle by his side. The sneaky machine was about to get away . . . but then Blaze zoomed up behind him!

"Aww, no," Crusher groaned. "He's gonna try to get the tools back!" The big truck had an idea!

"I'll make a Slippery Banana Launcher to stop him!" Crusher's contraption sent bananas flying through the air and splattering all over the street!

Every time Blaze and AJ tried to drive up the hill, the bananas made them slip back down.

Blaze had a plan. "See all those little bumps in the road? They give my tires something to grab on to," he said to AJ. "That's friction. But my tires can't grab on to squished bananas because they're too slippery."

"We need to keep our tires on the bumps in the road, where there's more friction," said AJ.

Blaze and AJ carefully steered around the squished bananas to the top of the hill!

Crusher and Pickle raced onto a boat and escaped across a bay.

"Lug nuts!" exclaimed Blaze. "We're gonna need a really fast boat to catch up!"

"Those waves make it hard to go fast," said AJ. "When they knock into the boat, they cause friction and slow you down."

"We want less friction so our boat can slide really fast across the water," said Blaze.

That gave AJ an idea.

The best buddies set to work turning Blaze into a hydrofoil, a special kind of boat that rides *above* the waves.

"First I need a hull so I can float," said Blaze. "Then I need a propeller, which will spin really fast and push the boat forward. And I've got to have foils to lift the boat off the water."

"Whoa! Blaze, you look awesome!" exclaimed AJ. "Hang on, AJ! This hydrofoil is ready for action!" said Blaze. He splashed into the water and easily zoomed over the choppy waves after Crusher and Pickle.

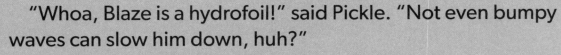

"Whoa, Blaze is a hydrofoil!" said Pickle. "Not even bumpy waves can slow him down, huh?"

But Crusher had another idea.

"I just thought of something that will definitely stop Blaze," said Crusher. "He'll never get past a chomping Shark Bot!"

"That Shark Bot is a big problem," said AJ when he spotted it, "and we need to find a solution!"

"We've got to figure out how to make him stop chomping," added Blaze. "And the only way to do that is to feed him something he can't chomp!"

Blaze and AJ found a metal pipe and tossed it at the Shark Bot, which fell apart. They had found a solution!

Crusher and Pickle made their way back onto land. They didn't know that Blaze and AJ weren't far behind them.

"Ha, ha! The tools are all mine!" Crusher said. But he accidentally dropped the toolbox down a large hill. Then he heard Blaze approaching.

"Quick, Pickle! We've got to get the toolbox before Blaze does!" The two trucks raced down the hill.

"We have to beat Crusher to that toolbox!" said Blaze when he and AJ reached the top of the hill. "Looks like our only chance to beat him is to put something slippery on the ground so there's no friction and we can slide to the bottom!"

"Hey, Blaze, what about this?" suggested AJ.

"One of Crusher's Super-Slippery Bananas—that's perfect!" replied Blaze.

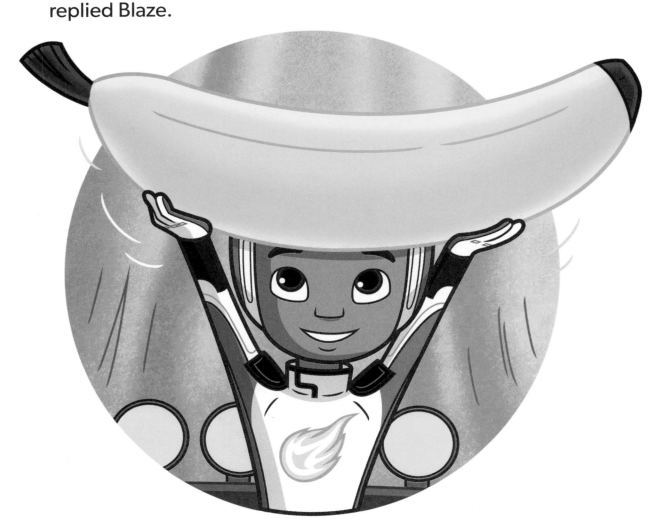

Blaze smashed the banana with one of his giant tires! It splattered and made a slippery, slimy trail. Then they jumped on the gooey path and quickly slid down to the bottom. They beat Crusher and Pickle!

"We got the tools!" exclaimed Blaze!

"All right! Nice slidin', Blaze!" added AJ as Crusher slid down the slippery trail and smashed into a pile of pinecones behind them.

"I can't believe those guys beat me—again!" cried Crusher.

"Uh, Crusher?" said Pickle. "I think your exhaust pipe might be broken."

"My exhaust pipe is broken?" Crusher asked.

"Crusher, I think you're forgetting that we know someone who can fix you," Blaze reminded him. "Gabby!"

"She just needs to get her tools back . . . ," said AJ.

"Oh, right," Crusher replied sheepishly.

Gabby and the rest of the Monster Machines
cheered when they saw Blaze arrive at the garage.
"Blaze! AJ! You got my tools back!" said Gabby.
"Now I can finally fix everyone! Even you, Crusher!"

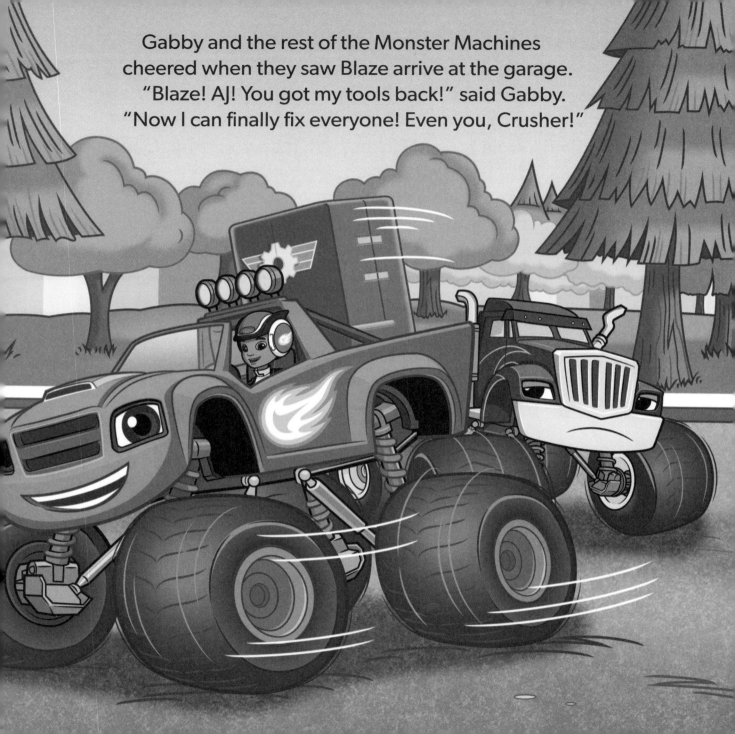

Gabby used her tools to fix all the Monster Machines, including Crusher.

"Well, look at that! Your exhaust pipe looks good as new," said Pickle.

"Ha! It does, doesn't it?" said Crusher. "All righty, then—let's get out of here!"

"Uh, hold on, Crusher," said Pickle. "What do you say to Gabby for fixing you?"

"Thank you," grumbled Crusher.

"There! Was that so hard?" asked Pickle, and he and the newly repaired machines went for a drive.